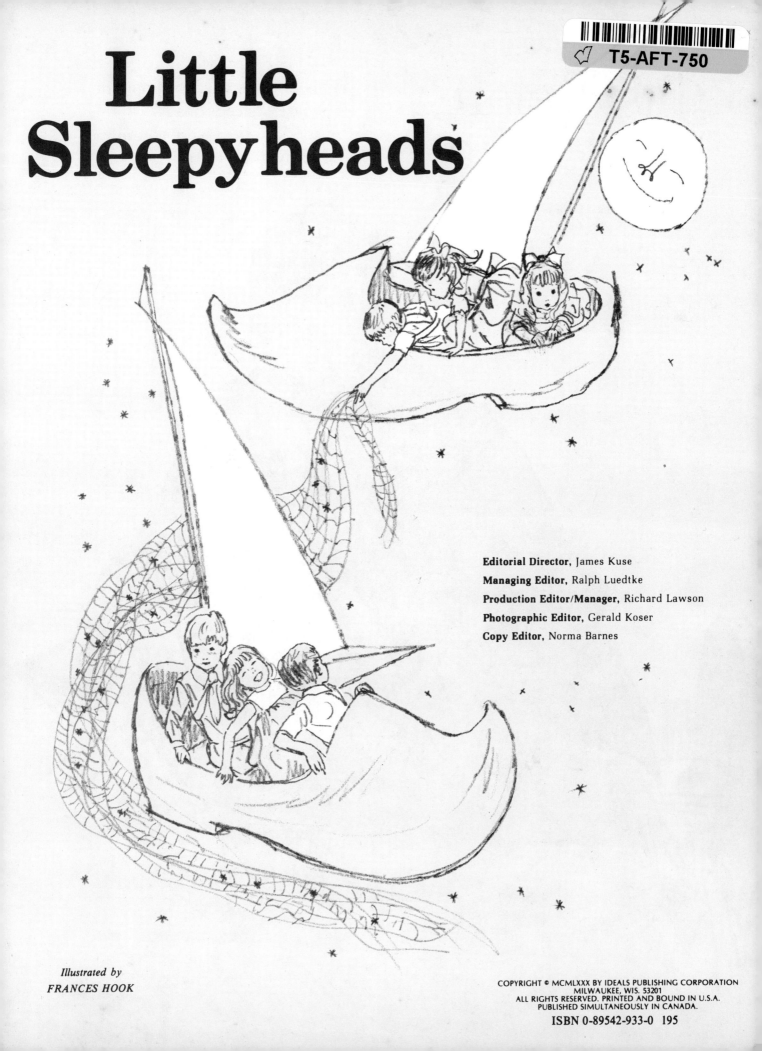

Little Sleepyheads

Editorial Director, James Kuse

Managing Editor, Ralph Luedtke

Production Editor/Manager, Richard Lawson

Photographic Editor, Gerald Koser

Copy Editor, Norma Barnes

Illustrated by
FRANCES HOOK

ISBN 0-89542-933-0 195

Just Before... ...Bed-Time

Garnett Ann Schultz

This book is filled with gladness
For little "sleepy heads,"
A special poem—for you alone—
Before you go to bed.

A precious bit of childhood,
A dream to bring delight,
To tell you, dear, that we are near,
Until the morning's light.

This book is for together-times,
That you and I might share,
For every night of all the year—
You'll always find it here.

A book of bedtime happiness,
We'll read and read again,
A bit of joy, for girl or boy,
Before we tuck you in.

Hey, Diddle, Diddle

Hey! diddle, diddle,
The cat and the fiddle,

The cow jumped over
The moon.

The little dog laughed
To see such sport

And the dish ran away
With the spoon!

Mother Goose

Mary Had A Little Lamb

Sarah Josepha Hale

Mary had a little lamb,
Its fleece was white as snow,
And everywhere that Mary went
The lamb was sure to go.

*It followed her to school one day;
That was against the rule.
It made the children laugh and play
To see a lamb at school.*

And so the teacher turned it out,
But still it lingered near
And waited patiently about
Till Mary did appear.

*And then it ran to her and laid
Its head upon her arm,
As if it said, "I'm not afraid . . .
You'll keep me from all harm."*

"What makes the lamb love Mary so?"
The eager children cry.
"Why, Mary loves the lamb, you know,"
The teacher did reply.

If You Never Talked with Fairies

Elsie Melchert Fowler

If you never talked with fairies,
If you never heard them tell
All about their hidden houses
In a little, flowered dell,

How they curtain all their windows
　With pale cobweb lace so fine,
How they paint their walls with moonbeams
　(When we're all asleep at nine,)

If you never heard them singing
　With the baby frogs at night,
While silver stars are watching
　And twinkling with delight,

If you never . . . must I say it,
　For it's true, so I've been told . . .
If you never talked with fairies
　You were always, always old!

My Shadow

Robert Louis Stevenson

I have a little shadow that goes in and out with me,
And what can be the use of him is more than I can see.

He is very, very like me from the heels up to the head,
And I see him jump before me when I jump into my bed.

The funniest thing about him is the way he likes to grow ..
Not at all like proper children, which is always very slow;

For he sometimes shoots up taller like an India-rubber ball,
And he sometimes gets so little that there's none of him at all.

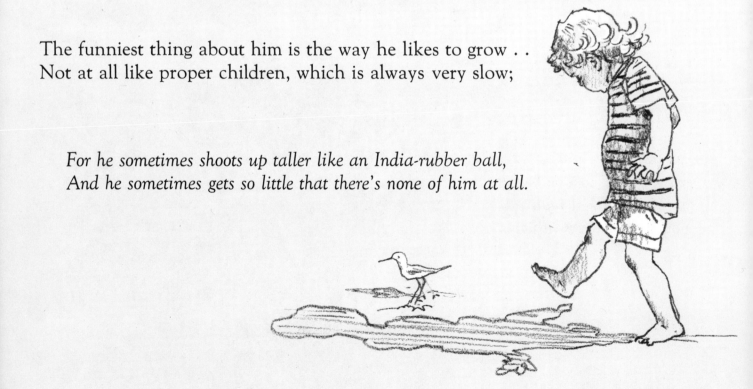

He hasn't got a notion of how children ought to play,
And can only make a fool of me in every sort of way.

He stays so close beside me, he's a coward you can see . . .
I'd think shame to stick to nursie as that shadow sticks to me!

One morning very early, before the sun was up,
I rose and found the shining dew on every buttercup,

But my lazy little shadow, like an errant sleepyhead,
Had stayed at home behind me and was fast asleep in bed!

From A CHILD'S GARDEN OF VERSES
by Robert Louis Stevenson
(Charles Scribner's Sons 1917)

The Land of Counterpane

Robert Louis Stevenson

When I was sick and lay a-bed,
I had two pillows at my head,
And all my toys beside me lay
To keep me happy all the day.

And sometimes for an hour or so
I watched my leaden soldiers go,
With different uniforms and drills,
Among the bed-clothes, through the hills;

And sometimes sent my ships in fleets
All up and down among the sheets;
Or brought my trees and houses out,
And planted cities all about.

I was the giant great and still
That sits upon the pillow-hill,
And sees before him, dale and plain,
The pleasant Land of Counterpane.

From A CHILD'S GARDEN OF VERSES
by Robert Louis Stevenson
(Charles Scribner's Sons 1895)

Daisies

Frank Dempster Sherman

At evening when I go to bed
I see the stars shine overhead.
They are the little daisies white
That dot the meadow of the night.

And often while I'm dreaming so,
Across the sky the moon will go.
It is a lady, sweet and fair,
Who comes to gather daisies there.

For, when at morning I arise,
There's not a star left in the skies,
She's picked them all and dropped them down
Into the meadows of the town.

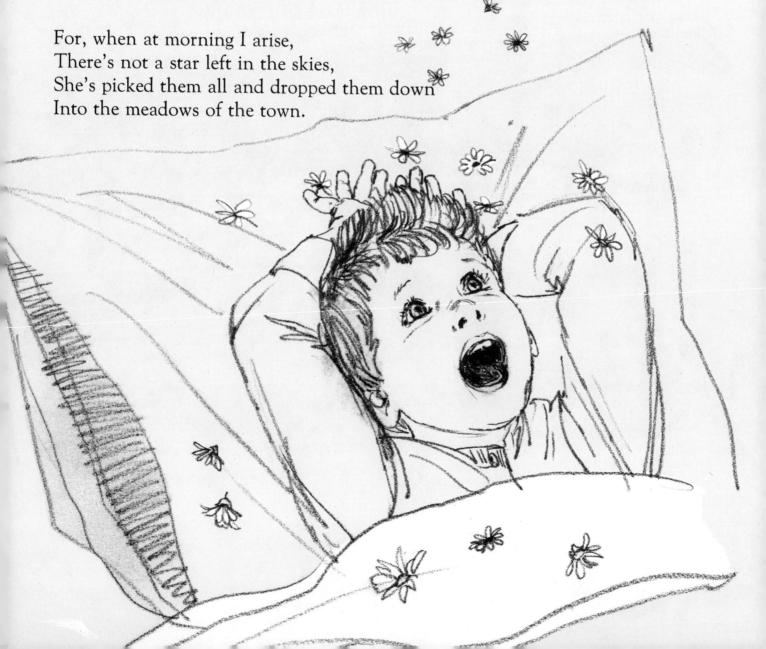

Wee, Willie Winkie

William Miller

Wee Willie Winkie
Runs through the town,
Upstairs and downstairs
In his nightgown.

Tapping at the window,
Crying at the lock,
"Are the babies in their bed?
For it's now eight o'clock."

There Was A Crooked Man

There was a crooked man,

and he went a crooked mile.

He found a crooked sixpence

against a crooked stile.

He bought a crooked cat

which caught a crooked mouse,

And they all lived together
in a little crooked house!

Mother Goose

Weather Song

When the weather is wet,
We must not fret.

When the weather is cold,
We must not scold.

When the weather is warm,
We must not storm . . .

But be thankful together,
Whatever the weather.

Monday's Child

Monday's child is fair of face,
Tuesday's child is full of grace,

Wednesday's child is full of woe,
Thursday's child has far to go,

Friday's child is loving, giving,
Saturday's child works hard for a living;

And a child that is born on the Sabbath day
Is fair and wise and good and gay.

Mother Goose

Thirty Days Hath September

Thirty days hath September,
April, June and November;

All the rest have thirty-one
Except the second month alone
Which hath but twenty-eight in fine
Till leap year makes it twenty-nine.

One, Two, Buckle My Shoe

One, two, buckle my shoe,
Three, four, shut the door,
Five, six, pick up sticks,
Seven, eight, lay them straight,
Nine, ten, a good fat hen.

Eleven, twelve, dig and delve,
Thirteen, fourteen, maids a-courting,
Fifteen, sixteen, maids in the kitchen,
Seventeen, eighteen, maids are waiting,
Nineteen, twenty, my plate's empty.

Mother Goose

There Was Once a Puffin

Florence Page Jaques

Oh, there once was a puffin
Just the shape of a muffin,
And he lived on an island
In the
      bright
          blue sea!

He ate little fishes,
That were most delicious,
And he had them for supper
And he
      had
         them for tea!

But this poor little puffin,
He couldn't play nothin',
For he hadn't anybody
To play
      with
         at all!

So he sat on his island,
And he cried for awhile, and
He felt very lonely
And he
        felt
            very small.

Then along came the fishes,
And they said, "If you wishes,
You can have us for playmates,
Instead
        of
            for tea!"

So they now play together,
In all sorts of weather,
And the puffin eats pancakes,
Like you
            and
                like me!

Jack and Jill

Jack and Jill went up the hill
To fetch a pail of water.

Jack fell down and broke his crown
And Jill came tumbling after.

Up Jack got, and home did trot
As fast as he could caper;

Went to bed and bound his head
With vinegar and brown paper.

Mother Goose

Humpty Dumpty

Humpty Dumpty
Sat on a wall,

Humpty Dumpty
Had a great fall . . .

All the King's horses
And all the King's men,

Could not put Humpty Dumpty
Together again!

The Duck and the Kangaroo

Edward Lear

Said the Duck to the Kangaroo,
"Good gracious! How you hop
Over the fields, and the water, too,
As if you never would stop!
My life is a bore in this nasty pond,
And I long to go out in the world beyond.
I wish I could hop like you,"
Said the Duck to the Kangaroo.

"Please give me a ride on your back,"
Said the Duck to the Kangaroo.
"I would sit quite still, and say nothing but 'Quack'
The whole of the long day through,
And we'd go the Dee, and the Jelly Bo Lee,
Over the land, and over the sea.
Please take me a ride! Oh, do!"
Said the Duck to the Kangaroo.

Said the Kangaroo to the Duck,
"This requires some little reflection.
Perhaps, on the whole, it might bring me luck,
And there seems but one objection:
Which is, if you'll let me speak so bold,
Your feet are unpleasantly wet and cold,
And would probably give me the roo—
Matiz," said the Kangaroo.

Said the Duck, "As I sat on the rocks,
I have thought over that completely,
And I bought four pairs of worsted socks
Which fit my web-feet neatly,
And to keep out the cold, I've bought a cloak,
And every day a cigar I'll smoke;
All to follow my own dear true
Love of a Kangaroo."

Said the Kangaroo, "I'm ready,
All in the moonlight pale;
But to balance me well, dear Duck, sit steady,
And quite at the end of my tail."
So away they went with a hop and a bound,
And they hopped the whole world three times round.
And who so happy, oh! who,
As the Duck and the Kangaroo?

The Rainbow Fairies

Lizzie M. Hadley

Two little clouds one summer's day
Went flying through the sky.
They went so fast they bumped their heads,
And both began to cry.

Old Father Sun looked out and said,
"Oh, never mind, my dears,
I'll send my little fairy folk
To dry your falling tears."

One fairy came in violet,
And one in indigo,
In blue, green, yellow, orange, red . . .
They made a pretty row.

They wiped the cloud tears all away,
And then, from out the sky,
Upon a line the sunbeams made,
They hung their gowns to dry.

Our sincere thanks to the author
whose address we were unable to locate

The Little Elf

John Kendrick Bangs

I met a little Elf-man, once,
Down where the lilies blow.

*I asked him why he was so small,
And why he didn't grow.*

He slightly frowned, and with his eye
He looked me through and through.

*"I'm quite as big for me," said he,
"As you are big for you."*

*From A ST. NICHOLAS ANTHOLOGY:
The Early Years, edited by Burton C. Frye,
© 1969. Reprinted by permission of
Prentice-Hall, Inc., Englewood Cliffs, New Jersey.*

Mr. Nobody

I know a funny little man,
As quiet as a mouse,
Who does the mischief that is done
In everybody's house.

There's no one ever sees his face,
And yet we all agree
That every plate we break was cracked
By Mr. Nobody.

'Tis he who always tears our books;
Who leaves our doors ajar.
He pulls the bottoms from our shirts,
And scatters pins afar.

That squeaking door will always squeak,
For, prithee, don't you see,
We leave the oiling to be done
By Mr. Nobody.

He puts damp wood upon the fire,
That kettles cannot boil;
His are the feet that bring in mud,
And all the carpets soil.

The papers always are mislaid.
Who had them last but he?
There's no one tosses them about
But Mr. Nobody.

The finger-marks upon the door
By none of us are made.
We never leave the blinds unclosed,
To let the curtains fade.

The ink we never spill; the boots
That lying round you see
Are not our boots: they all belong
To Mr. Nobody!

Wynken, Blynken, and Nod

Eugene Field

Wynken, Blynken, and Nod one night
Sailed off in a wooden shoe . . .
Sailed on a river of crystal light,
Into a sea of dew.

"Where are you going, and what do you wish?"
The old moon asked the three.
"We have come to fish for the herring fish
That live in this beautiful sea.
Nets of silver and gold have we!"
Said Wynken, Blynken, and Nod.

The old moon laughed and sang a song,
As they rocked in the wooden shoe,
And the wind that sped them all night long
Ruffled the waves of dew.
The little stars were the herring fish
That lived in the beautiful sea.
"Now cast your nets wherever you wish . . .
Never afeared are we!"
So cried the stars to the fishermen three,
Wynken, Blynken, and Nod.

*All night long their nets they threw
To the stars in the twinkling foam . . .
Then down from the skies came the wooden shoe,
Bringing the fishermen home.
'Twas all so pretty a sail, it seemed
As if it could not be,
And some folks thought 'twas a dream they'd dreamed
Of sailing that beautiful sea.
But I shall name you the fishermen three,
Wynken, Blynken, and Nod.*

Wynken and Blynken are two little eyes,
And Nod is a little head,
And the wooden shoe that sailed the skies
Is a wee one's trundle bed.
So shut your eyes while Mother sings
Of wonderful sights that be,
And you shall see the beautiful things
As you rock in the misty sea
Where the old shoe rocked the fishermen three,
Wynken, Blynken, and Nod.

From POEMS OF CHILDHOOD
by Eugene Field
(Charles Scribner's Sons)

Twinkle, Twinkle, Little Star

Jane Taylor

Twinkle, twinkle, little star,
How I wonder what you are!
Up above the world so high,
Like a diamond in the sky.

When the blazing sun is gone,
When he nothing shines upon,
Then you show your little light,
Twinkle, twinkle, all the night.

Then the traveler in the dark
Thanks you for your tiny spark.
He could not tell which way to go
If you did not twinkle so.

In the dark blue sky you keep,
And often through my curtains peep,
For you never shut your eye
Till the sun is in the sky.

As your bright and tiny spark
Lights the traveler in the dark,
Though I know not what you are,
Twinkle, twinkle, little star.